P9-BZH-907

SCOOBY-DOO!™

The Big Bad Blizzard

By Gail Herman
Illustrated by Duendes del Sur

SCHOLASTIC INC.

New York Toronto London Auckland Sydney
Mexico City New Delhi Hong Kong Buenos Aires

No part of this publication may be reproduced, stored in a retrieval system, or transmitted in any form or by any means, electronic, mechanical, photocopying, recording, or otherwise, without written permission of the publisher. For information regarding permission, write to Scholastic Inc., Attention: Permissions Department, 557 Broadway, New York, NY 10012.

ISBN 13: 978-0-439-78810-6
ISBN 10: 0-439-78810-2
Copyright © 2007 Hanna-Barbera.
SCOOBY-DOO and all related characters and elements are trademarks of and © Hanna-Barbera.
Used under license by Scholastic Inc. Published by Scholastic Inc.
SCHOLASTIC and associated logos are trademarks and/or registered trademarks of Scholastic Inc.

Designed by Michael Massen

12   11   10   9   8   7   6   5   4   3   7   8   9   10/0

Printed in the U.S.A.
First printing, September 2007

Scooby-Doo, Shaggy, and the gang were going skiing.

"Like, that mountain is tall," said Shaggy. "Too tall to ski down. Right, Scoob?"

"Right, Raggy!"

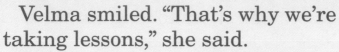

Velma smiled. "That's why we're taking lessons," she said.
"So we can learn how to ski down the mountain safely," Fred added.

"Hi!" A man skidded to a stop. "I'm Todd, your teacher."

"Then teach me how to take these off." Shaggy jiggled his skis. "We need to get some chow."

"If you finish your lesson, you can eat there."
Todd pointed to the top of the mountain.

A restaurant sign flashed: TIP TOP TREATS! ALL
YOU CAN EAT!

"Still want to take off your skis?" Daphne teased.
"Ro way!" Scooby barked.

Todd led the gang past the ski lift. "We'll start here," he said. "It's for beginners."

"But, but," Shaggy stammered. "That doesn't go to the restaurant!"

While Velma, Fred, and Daphne waited in line, Shaggy and Scooby sneaked back to the ski lift.

"Jump on up, good buddy," said Shaggy.
"Next stop, lunch!"

"Stop! It's too dangerous!" shouted Todd.
But Shaggy and Scooby didn't hear him.
Their stomachs were growling too loudly.

Snow began to fall as Shaggy and Scooby rode past the Bunny Run . . .

BUNNY RUN

. . . past the Bear Run,
and the Big Bear Run.

One by one, skiers got off the lift.
Finally, Shaggy and Scooby reached the top.
"Like, jump!" said Shaggy. The two leaped.
They slipped and slid.

The snow almost covered a sign that read:
BLIZZARD ALERT! ALL SLOPES CLOSED! The
other skiers turned back.

Some skiers yelled at Shaggy and Scooby, "Turn back!"

"Did you hear something, Scoob old pal?"

Scooby shook snow out of his ears. Then he shrugged, and peered around.

The snow fell harder and faster. It was a blizzard!

"Like, where is everybody?" asked Shaggy. "And where's that all-you-can-eat place?"

Something strange was going on.
Shaggy wiped snow from a sign.
"Monster Run," he read.
"Monster?" he cried. "RUN!"

"There's only one way to go, good buddy," Shaggy yelled above the wind. "That's down!"

Shaggy and Scooby took one step. Then another.

"We're doing it!" said Shaggy. "Who needs lessons? Right, Scoob? Scoob?"

Scooby-Doo didn't answer. He was staring straight ahead.

A giant snow creature floated toward them. Its long arms swung back and forth.

"Row ronster!" Scooby shouted.

"Ro!" Scooby cried. "Row ronsters!"
Shaggy counted two, three, four!
Their loud moans echoed in the wind.
"Oooob! Aaggg! Oooob! Aaggg!"

Shaggy and Scooby clutched each other. Their skis bumped and banged.

"Like, whoa!" said Shaggy as they tumbled down . . . down . . . down. Straight into the biggest monsters yet.

The creatures bent closer. They reached out
with long, sharp arms.

"Zoinks! Let's get out of here!" Shaggy cried.

Shaggy and Scooby tried to run.
Instead, they rolled and rolled.
"OOOOOB! AAAAAAG!" The monsters
moaned, following close behind.

Splat! The Scooby Shaggy snowball hit
the bottom.
Monster hands scooped away the snow.
"We're goners!" Shaggy groaned.

"Oob? Aag?"
Shaggy looked at Scooby.
"Like, the monster sounds a little like . . ."
The snow monster peeled off a ski mask.
"Scooby? Shaggy?" Velma said more clearly.

Velma took off her giant ski gloves and grinned. Velma wasn't a monster. But what about the others?

"Watch out!" Shaggy shouted.

"Three snow monsters are chasing us!"

"That's Todd — and Fred and Daphne," said Velma.

"What about those monster arms?" Shaggy asked.

"They're just ski poles," Velma explained.

"And those monster shapes?" Shaggy asked.

"Backpacks covered in snow," Velma replied.

Todd opened his backpack.

"Rot chocolate!" said Scooby. "Rot dogs!"

"You kept running away!" Todd said. "But we were trying to help."

"What about those really scary creatures?
And that sign about monsters?" asked Shaggy.
"Monster Run is the name of the trail,"
Daphne said.
"And those other monsters are just trees,"
Fred added.

"Like, phew!" said Shaggy, digging into the hot dogs. "Now we can eat!"

Soon, the snow had stopped.

Shaggy pointed to the mountaintop. The Tip Top Treats sign flashed in the sunshine.

"Ready for another run?" he asked Scooby.